Emma Thomson's
felicity Wishes®

fairy fluster

By Emma Thomson and Helen Bailey

Illustrated by Emma Thomson

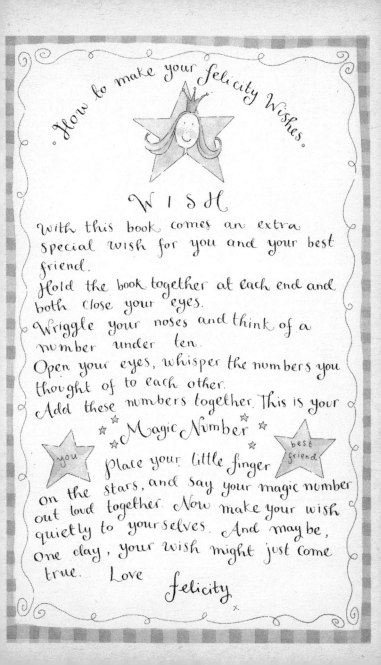

How to make your felicity Wishes

W I S H

With this book comes an extra special wish for you and your best friend.

Hold the book together at each end and both close your eyes.

Wriggle your noses and think of a number under ten.

Open your eyes, whisper the numbers you thought of to each other.

Add these numbers together. This is your

✶ *Magic Number* ✶

you

best friend

Place your little finger on the stars, and say your magic number out loud together. Now make your wish quietly to yourselves. And maybe, one day, your wish might just come true. Love

felicity

x

FELICITY WISHES®
Written by Emma Thomson and Helen Bailey
Illustrated by Emma Thomson

Felicity Wishes © 2000 Emma Thomson
Licensed by White Lion Publishing.

Felicity Wishes: Fairy Fluster © 2004 Emma Thomson and Helen Bailey
Illustrations copyright © 2002 Emma Thomson

'Cooking Disaster' first published in Felicity Wishes: Spooky Sleepover
© 2002 Emma Thomson and Helen Bailey
'Decorating Disaster' first published in Felicity Wishes: Fashion Fiasco
© 2002 Emma Thomson and Helen Bailey

First published in Great Britain in 2002 by Hodder Children's Books
This edition published 2004

A Catalogue record for this book is available from the British Library

ISBN 0 340 88228X

Printed and bound in Great Britain by Clays Ltd, St Ives plc.

Our grateful thanks to Avocet Typeset, Saxon, Norske Skog Union, Enso Publication Papers,
Paper Management Services, Clays Ltd and Kadocourt

CONTENTS

Cooking Crisis

Polly's Birthday
CAKES

• Double choc chip
  surprise
  3 layers →

• Fairy Cakes
  (extra light) →

• Flapjacks
  really gooey ones! →

• Cherry cookies +

Felicity Wishes and her friends were
making their way home from school.
They were talking about the lessons
they'd had that day.

Suddenly, Felicity remembered
something *much* more exciting.

"Polly! There's only a couple of
days left until your birthday and you
still haven't decided whether or not
to have a party!"

Holly, who had been flying along
while trying to read a magazine
at the same time, crashed into

Daisy, who had stopped to smell some pink roses.

"I've been too busy to even think about my birthday," Polly told Felicity, as she helped untangle Holly and Daisy. "I suppose I should do *something*."

"Leave it to me!" said Felicity brightly. "I'll make you a yummy birthday cake. In fact, *lots* of scrummy birthday cakes!"

The fairies looked at each other with raised eyebrows and wide eyes. It wasn't that Felicity didn't cook. She *loved* to cook. It was just that she never stuck to a recipe! Sometimes she forgot to read the recipe all the way through before starting, or found she didn't have all the ingredients, or forgot to switch the oven on. Something *always* seemed to go wrong.

Felicity saw her friends looking at

her in an 'are you sure this is
idea?' kind of way.

"Don't worry!" she said. "Come
my house on Saturday at four o'clock
for a birthday tea!"

With a hop, skip
and a flip of her
wings, Felicity
flew off to plan
Polly's birthday tea.

"I'll pop round
early," said
Daisy to the
others. "*Someone* has
got to keep an eye on her!"

* * *

All day on Friday during school,
Felicity thought about what she was
going to bake.

"Are you *sure* you want to do this,
Felicity?" asked Polly, after Felicity
had questioned her for the hundredth

time about whether she preferred jam or cream, or both, in a sponge cake. "I'm happy to go to Ice-Cream Dreams if it's too much bother."

"It's all under control!" Felicity told Polly, writing down another cake idea on her ever-increasing list.

* * *

Felicity had taken a big pile of cookery books to bed with her and had marked the recipes with little slips of pink paper. It had taken her ages to fall asleep and, when she finally did, she dreamt she'd fallen into a giant bowl of cake mixture and eaten too much to climb out!

When she woke the next day, not only was it later than she had planned, but all the little pink slips of paper had fallen out of the cookery books, as she'd fallen asleep with them on her bed.

"Never mind," she thought to

herself. "I'm sure I can remember the recipes. I've read them so many times!"

She looked at the list of cakes to bake. She would have to work quickly if she was to get everything finished by four o'clock!

* * *

Felicity switched on the oven.

"I'll leave it to heat up for ten minutes," she thought to herself. "Then I'll start making the chocolate birthday cake."

She wandered out into the garden, just as Holly was flying past. Seeing Felicity, she stopped to chat.

"I'm off to have my hair done,"

said Holly. "I thought I might try Star Treatment for a change."

Holly and Felicity were still chatting about hairstyles when Holly wrinkled her nose.

"Can you smell burning?" she asked Felicity. "Have you got anything in the oven?"

"Not yet," replied Felicity. "I wonder if someone is having a bonfire?"

The burning smell became stronger and stronger.

"Are you *sure* it's not something you're cooking?" said Holly, setting off down the path to Felicity's house.

"It's really not me!" laughed Felicity, following her. "I've nothing in the oven to burn!"

They trooped into Felicity's kitchen. Thick black smoke was pouring from behind the oven door.

"Don't open the door!" shouted Holly. "Turn off the oven and open

the windows!"

Holly and Felicity stood staring
at the smouldering oven. When the
smoke had died down, Felicity
carefully opened the door and
peered inside. Wearing
a huge pair of oven
gloves she reached
in and brought out
a small, black object.

"What is it?" asked Holly, poking it with a wooden spoon.

"I think it *was* a gingerbread fairy. I must have left it in the oven by mistake last time I baked!" said Felicity. "Look, you can just about make out the outline of her crown!"

* * *

Holly left to go to Star Treatment and Felicity began to make the chocolate cake. The oven was still very hot.

"Most people have to wait for the oven to heat up before they start cooking," she thought to herself as she stirred the cake mixture. "Trust me to have to wait for it to cool down!"

The cake mixture was creamy and golden. Time to add the chocolate powder! She looked in the cupboard but couldn't see any.

"I *know* it's in here," she thought as she peered at the tins and packets.

Eventually, at the back, she found what she was looking for. But, when she prised open the lid, instead of seeing a loose mound of chocolate powder, all she saw was a solid, brown lump. Felicity looked at the 'Use By' date on the bottom of the tin. Two years ago!

She tried chipping away at the lump with the edge of her wand, but all she managed to do was break a tip off the star.

Hot water didn't even *begin* to dissolve it, and banging the tin on the floor to free the chocolate only dented it.

Felicity glanced at the clock. The morning was nearly over! There wasn't time to go to Little Blossoming for more chocolate powder. She'd have to turn the mixture into fairy cakes.

She was sure Polly wouldn't mind.

Just as she was about to spoon the mixture into pretty paper cases she decided to add more self-raising flour, just for luck.

✳ ✳ ✳

The fairy cake mixture was rising beautifully in the oven, so Felicity began to make the flapjacks.

"Everything is going according to plan!" she thought, as she smoothed the gooey mixture on to two large, silver baking trays.

"This is better," she thought, as she took the golden fairy cakes out of the oven and left them on a rack to cool.

Putting the flapjacks in the oven, she set the timer for fifteen minutes and, as there were no more bowls left to make the cherry cookies, began to do the washing up, her arms elbow deep in frothy bubbles.

Out of the corner of her eye she

noticed something about the rack of
cooling fairy cakes had changed.
Instead of twelve cakes, there were
now only eleven. She was *sure* she had
filled twelve cases, but perhaps she
had been mistaken. A moment later,
she looked again. This time there
were only ten!

Puzzled, Felicity stared at the
cakes. In front of her eyes, one by
one, the cakes rose up and floated
out of the open window and across
the garden.

She had put so much self-raising flour in the mixture they were floating away as they cooled!

Felicity rushed out into the garden and ran down the path, but it was too late. The cakes were heading off over Little Blossoming.

Just when Felicity thought it couldn't get any worse, she remembered the flapjacks. The kitchen timer had gone off, but Felicity had been right at the bottom of the garden, so hadn't heard it!

Dashing back into the house, she opened the oven door and pulled out two trays of solid, burnt flapjacks, stuck firmly to their tins.

Felicity sat at the kitchen table and buried her head in her hands.

"What *am* I going to do?" she wailed.

"Go to the cake shop!" said a voice.

Felicity looked up to see Daisy staring at the chaos that surrounded her distraught fairy friend.

"What are you doing here?" asked Felicity, drying her eyes on the oven glove.

"There's a trail of fairy cakes floating over Little Blossoming," said Daisy, prodding the burnt flapjacks. "I guessed they came from your house."

* * *

Felicity agreed with Daisy that if the birthday tea was to go ahead, there was no choice but to go to the cake shop, but when they arrived at The Sticky Bun, there wasn't a single cake to be seen.

"Aren't there *any* cakes left?" Felicity asked the shop assistant desperately.

The assistant shook her head.

"Someone came in and bought every cake, bun and biscuit we had."

* * *

Daisy and Felicity left the shop and sat underneath a huge tree.

Felicity had one last idea.

"Daisy, would you try and wish for some cakes for me?" She hesitated for a moment, remembering her fairy motto. "You would be using your wishes for the good of others."

But Daisy didn't want to try.

"Remember when I tried to magic some scones in cookery class?" she asked Felicity. "They were as heavy and as hard as stones."

Holly claimed her toe still hurt from where a scone had fallen on it.

"Owww!" screeched Felicity.

"Yes, that's what Holly said," remembered Daisy.

"No, I mean, ouch, I've just been hit by a falling apple!"

The fairies looked up and realised they were sitting under an apple tree bursting with apples.

"Toffee apples!" exclaimed Felicity. "We can make Polly toffee apples!"

Daisy flew up into the tree and gently tapped on the branches with her wand, and Felicity stood below, holding out her skirt to catch the falling fruit.

"I don't suppose you've got any lollipop sticks?" asked Daisy.

"Hundreds!" said Felicity, remembering a drawer full of them at home. "I knew they'd come in handy one day!"

✳ ✳ ✳

When they got back to Felicity's kitchen they washed the apples, pushed in the lolly sticks and, after checking one of Felicity's recipe books, made a huge pot of sticky toffee mixture into which they dipped the apples.

"Thank goodness *something* has gone right!" said Felicity, admiring the rows of apples dripping with gleaming, glassy toffee.

It was nearly four o'clock! Soon Polly and Holly would be round.

Felicity and Daisy put out Polly's presents and cards on the table and filled jugs with lemonade.

Felicity's tummy began to rumble.

"In all the rush I forgot to have lunch!" she said to Daisy.

"Why not try a toffee apple?" said Daisy. "There are plenty of them!"

Felicity picked up one of the apples and sunk her teeth through the sticky toffee and into the crispy apple. But when she tried to take another bite she found that the toffee was so sticky her teeth had become stuck. The harder she tried to pull the toffee apple from her mouth, the more the toffee set around her teeth.

"Is that nice?" asked Daisy, looking at the apples and not noticing Felicity, wide-eyed and pointing frantically at her mouth.

Felicity let out a muffled noise which sounded like "Mmmmm".

"In that case, I'll try one myself," said Daisy. As she bit into the sticky apple she turned and saw Felicity, her mouth stuck to the toffee apple, trying to tell her not to eat one. Too late!

The fairies tried to pull the apples out but, every time they did, they felt as if their teeth were coming out.

The phone rang. Felicity picked it up.

"Uuh – ho," she said.

"Felicity! It's Polly. I'm going to be a little late. Are you all right?"

Felicity tried to say yes but it came out as "us".

Polly was worried now.

"Is Daisy there? Put me on to Daisy."

Felicity handed the phone to Daisy, who managed to make a series of muffled grunts and snorts before putting the phone down.

* * *

Polly came flying through the door at great speed.

She could not believe her eyes when she saw her two friends sitting at the kitchen table, silent, with two huge toffee apples stuck in their mouths.

As it was Felicity's kitchen and

involved Felicity's cooking, she didn't even ask how it had happened. Very gently, she tugged at the sticky apples in her friends' mouths, ignoring their yelps and carefully chipping away any bits of stuck toffee. Eventually, Daisy and Felicity were freed from their sticky apples.

"You're going to be a brilliant Tooth Fairy!" exclaimed Felicity, gulping down a glass of lemonade. "I thought my teeth were going to be stuck to that toffee apple for ever!"

"Thank goodness I stopped at The Sticky Bun for cakes!" said Holly, coming through the door with a box filled with the most yummy cakes and buns they had ever seen.

"It was *you*!" said Felicity to Holly. "You were the one who bought all the cakes! How did you know that I had had a bad cooking day?"

"I saw the fairy cakes flying across Little Blossoming this morning," said Holly, sticking some candles into one of the cakes. "I thought these might come in useful."

Polly saw Felicity's face crumple a little and put her arms around her.

"Holly buying cakes was a lovely gesture but" – she winked at Holly – "you trying to make them yourself for me is every bit as lovely. It's the thought that counts."

"Don't worry," said Felicity brightly, "I'll have it all under control next year!"

things given with
all your heart
are always lovely

even when they
go wrong!

Decorating
Disaster

Felicity Wishes and her friends
were lolling about on Felicity's bed,
planning what they were going to
do during the half-term break from
the School of Nine Wishes. They had
one week - just long enough to have
masses of fun!

"So," said Polly. "What's it to be? Shopping, shopping or more shopping?"

"I think," said Felicity, looking around her bedroom, "I'm going to re-decorate."

"Does it really need it?" asked Holly, flipping through a magazine without looking up. Decorating was not Holly's idea of fun at all. In fact, anything that required hard work sounded like a very bad idea indeed.

"*Need* doesn't come into it," said Felicity firmly. "I feel like a change."

"It does seem a shame to take down this lovely wallpaper," said Daisy. "It looks almost new to me."

Polly peered up at the ceiling. "I can see a bit of paper peeling - right there, in the corner."

"You see!" exclaimed Felicity triumphantly. "The room does need a make-over!"

"Just stick some glue on it!" said Holly, now becoming worried. "Glue it, let's go shopping and we'll think about decorating later!"

Felicity found some Soopa Doopa glue and Polly flew up to the ceiling to inspect the damage. In one corner there was a tiny piece of wallpaper which had come away from the wall.

"What's it to be, Felicity?" Polly shouted down. "Are we decorating or not?"

Felicity suddenly thought of all the work that needed to be done before the fun could start: moving furniture, taking down posters, removing the curtains, covering up the carpet, cleaning the walls. Even though her friends would help her, perhaps they *should* wait for the long summer holidays.

"Glue it!" shouted Felicity. "We'll leave the decorating for another time."

Holly let out a great sigh of relief and went back to reading magazines.

Polly squeezed a little Soopa Doopa glue out of the tube, but it wouldn't stop. The glue kept on spilling out of the tube in a huge sticky mess. On and on it oozed.

"The glue is going wild! I can't stop it coming out of the tube," she yelled down to her friends.

"Put some on the wallpaper, Pol!" shouted Felicity

"Put the cap back on!" shrieked Daisy.

Holly could feel a headache coming on.

* * *

The glue was getting everywhere. Everything Polly touched seemed to become covered with a layer of super sticky goo.

"I'm flying back down!" called Polly. "There's enough glue up here to stick glitter to every fairy wand in Little Blossoming!"

But as Polly flew down, there was the most tremendous ripping sound.

In amongst the sticky mess, a corner of Polly's right wing had become stuck to the wall. Streaming behind her like a huge paper cape was Felicity's wallpaper!

"Arghh…" shrieked Polly as she landed with a thump on the carpet, the wallpaper floating down and covering her in a huge gooey blanket.

"That's torn it!" said Holly, as the fairies rushed over to their crumpled friend.

With a large strip of wallpaper now covering Polly rather than the wall, there was nothing for it but to redecorate the room after all.

Everyone was already in such a mess that Daisy, Polly and Felicity decided to strip the rest of the wallpaper off the walls there and then, while Holly covered up the furniture with some large white sheets. They used the stars on their wands to prise away bits of wallpaper, then flew about the room pulling off strips like fat paper streamers.

When they had finished, they bundled all the mess into the bin, cleaned themselves up, had a cup of hot chocolate and set off for Do-It-Together to find something special to decorate Felicity's room with.

* * *

The shop was bustling with fairies
buying paint and paper of every
pattern and colour imaginable.

There was wallpaper with stripes
going up and stripes
going across.
Wallpaper
with big checks
you could play
noughts and
crosses on, and
wallpaper with
checks so tiny
they made

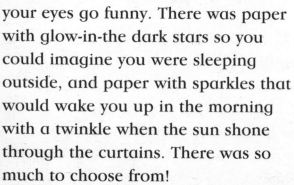

your eyes go funny. There was paper
with glow-in-the dark stars so you
could imagine you were sleeping
outside, and paper with sparkles that
would wake you up in the morning
with a twinkle when the sun shone
through the curtains. There was so
much to choose from!

Then Felicity saw a design she loved.

It was pale pink with enormous deep pink roses the size of dinner plates. Felicity thought it was gorgeous. The others weren't so sure.

"Don't you think the roses are a bit – well – *large*?" said Daisy, looking doubtfully at the design.

"They're humungous!" said Polly. "Far too large for your bedroom, Felicity. How about something more delicate?"

But Felicity was already hugging rolls of the paper. There was no dissuading her.

So the others gathered together some brushes, a bucket, some wallpaper paste and a hard hat for Holly (who was worried about her hair), then set off back to Felicity's house.

The first problem was finding a table long enough for the wallpaper. Holly suggested they used the ironing board which wasn't perfect but, if Daisy held the end of the paper carefully, might just work.

Polly opened the packet of wallpaper paste and sneezed so hard she added too much powder to the bucket of morning dew, making the paste as lumpy as porridge. Even her frantic whisking with the end of her wand didn't appear to make any difference.

Holly cut the wallpaper into a long strip, then put it on the ironing board. Felicity brushed the lumpy paste on to the back of the paper. With so much paste the wallpaper was very heavy and Daisy, Polly and Felicity had trouble lifting it up and flying to the ceiling to hang it.

Holly didn't like heights so she

shouted out instructions
from below.

"Up a bit, left a bit, right
a bit – hang!"

They fluttered up and
down smoothing out the
lumps, then stood back
to admire their handiwork.

The roses were, indeed,
humungous. Daisy had
been right, they were far
too big for Felicity's cosy
bedroom. But, more
worryingly, right in the
centre of the paper was
a huge bulge.

The friends looked at each
other, puzzled.

"What is that lump?" asked Holly.

"We smoothed the top, didn't we?" said Daisy to Felicity.

"And Polly and I did the bottom..." said Holly.

But no one had done the middle!

The fairies inspected the lump. It was large, and hard and brush-shaped.

"We've papered over the paste brush!" giggled Felicity.

The friends fell about laughing. Time to start again! But Felicity had had enough of the wallpaper with its huge roses and strange bulges.

"We've only done one sheet, it's been a disaster and I don't like the pattern after all. Let's take it back and get some paint instead."

"But Felicity," chorused her friends, "you've always said you think plain walls are boring!"

"A fairy can change her mind,

can't she?" Felicity replied, gathering
up the unused rolls of rose-patterned
paper before setting off to Do-It-
Together
again.

There was an even wider choice of
paint colours than there had been
of wallpaper patterns, but the fairies
knew exactly which colour Felicity
would choose. Pink. The question
was, which shade?

There was a lovely dusty pink the
same colour as Daisy's roses, a
fabulous deep pink which Felicity
knew would match her duvet
beautifully, a delicate light pink that
shimmered and was very special,
and a pink that reminded Felicity of
strawberry ice-cream.

"Oh, they're all yummy! I just don't know which one to choose," said Felicity, as she lined up the tins of paint. She closed her eyes and began, "I spy, with my closed eye..."

Daisy was horrified. "Felicity! You can't choose a colour like that!"

"It's the best way," said Felicity. "There's no such thing as a horrible pink, so whichever one I choose will be perfect."

She shut her eyes and began again, pointing randomly at the tins.

"I spy, with my closed eye, a colour beginning with P!" Felicity's finger stopped on a beautiful pinky lilac colour called 'Twilight Blush'.

It was perfect.

They each got a paint brush, a furry roller, and a pot of white paint for the skirting boards and, for the second time that day, headed back to Felicity's house to start decorating.

Painting was much more fun than papering and the fairies quickly covered the walls with a generous coat of 'Twilight Blush'. They also covered themselves with a layer of paint. The tin said "non-drip" but it didn't say "non-splash" and soon they all looked as if they had a bad case of chicken pox!

After Holly had painted the skirting boards white, they declared the room finished. It looked lovely.

"It's gorgeous, Felicity," said Polly.

"Your method of choosing a colour worked brilliantly after all," agreed Daisy.

Felicity was very quiet.

"Don't you like your new room?" asked Holly wearily. "*Please* tell me that you like it."

"I do," mumbled Felicity, looking down at her toes. What was a little white lie to save her friends' feelings?

But her friends knew her too well and her face said it all. Polly raised one eyebrow in an "are you sure?" kind of way.

"Honestly… I… er… do," said Felicity hesitantly. "It's just after wallpaper, the plain walls look a little… well… *plain*."

This time it was the turn of her friends to remain silent. They stared at her with their paint-splashed faces.

"I mean," said Felicity sensing her friends' despair and beginning to gabble, "I love the colour, but it's just a little… um… *boring*. It needs a pattern."

The fairies groaned. Holly threw herself on to the sheet-covered bed.

"It's at times like this that I'd really love to have graduated from the School of Nine Wishes," she moaned. "If I was a fully-qualified fairy I could just wave my magic wand and instantly transform your room to look however you wanted it. You could change your mind a hundred times and it wouldn't matter."

"Don't you think that might be thought of as a waste of a wish?" said Polly. One of the first lessons they had ever had at fairy school was the importance of using your wishes wisely. Polly wasn't sure that providing Felicity with the right wallpaper and paint counted as a wise wish.

Holly thought for a moment. "The fairy motto starts off saying: I promise to take good care of my wishes. To use them wisely for the good of others. We would be using a wish to help Felicity."

"Are you sure that would be your only reason, though? To help Felicity?" asked Polly, looking worried. "Don't forget, the motto goes on to say: Never to use them for my own gain. And to try my best to live by the Fairy Motto. By changing Felicity's room it means less work for us. Surely that's using a wish for our own gain?"

Daisy suddenly had an idea. "I know! We can still use our magic wands to transform Felicity's room, but without making a wish. Holly, have you got any white paint left?"

Holly handed over the tin to Daisy, who carefully dipped the end of the handle of her wand into the paint and dabbed it on to the pink wall. It made a perfect white spot. She then dipped one of the points of the star

in the paint and made eight tiny spots around the first larger spot. She stood back to let Polly, Holly and Felicity see. She had painted a small, white, perfectly formed flower.

"Daisy!" exclaimed Felicity hugging her friend. "That's brilliant! You are so clever."

Daisy turned a sort of 'Twilight Blush' colour and said, "Let's use our wands to cover all the walls."

So the four friends spent the rest of the day dipping and dabbing, painting flowers on the walls with their wands. When they finally finished and the last flower had been painted, Felicity couldn't have been happier. Not only did she have a beautiful pink bedroom, but one where each flower had been hand-painted with care by the friends she loved most. Every single flower would

always remind her how lucky she
was to have such good
fairy friends!

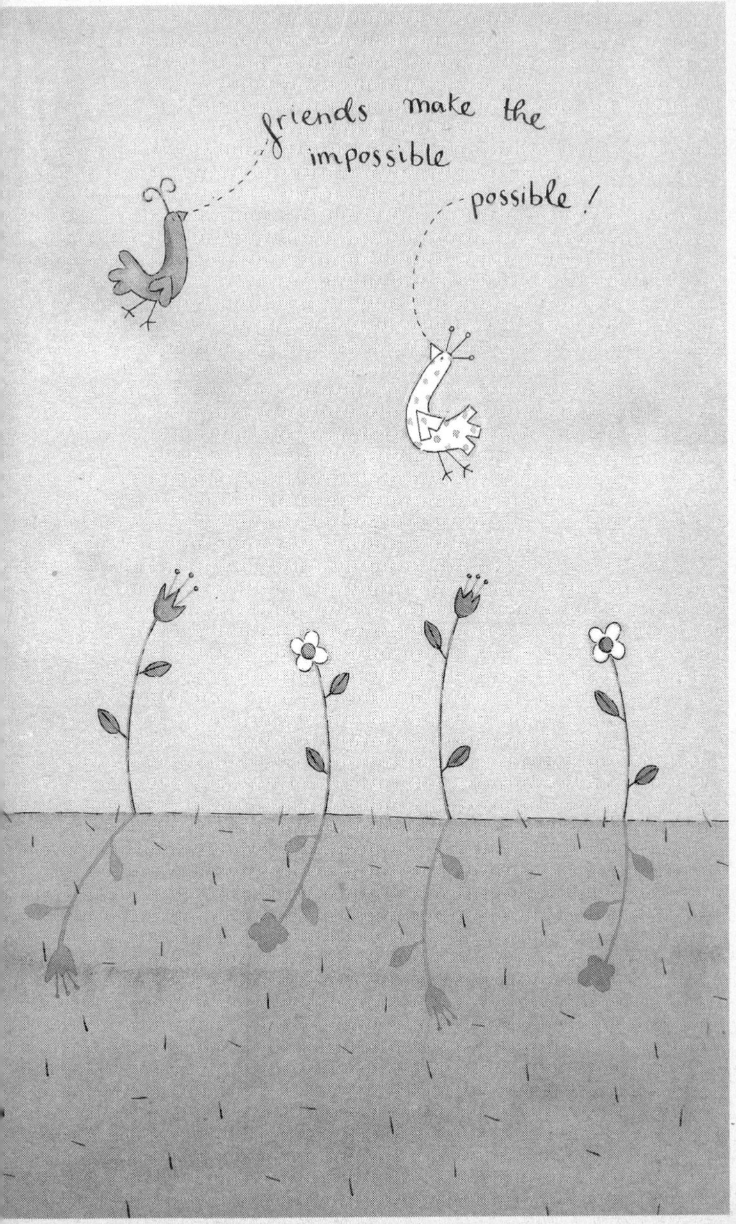
friends make the
impossible
possible!

If you enjoyed this book, why not try another of these fantastic novels from Emma Thomson?

Spooky Sleepover

Wand Wishes

Fashion Fiasco

Dancing Dreams

(available from WH Smith)

The Big Book of Magical Mishaps

(a bind-up of all four novels)

Also available in the Felicity Wishes range:

Felicity Wishes: Snowflakes and Sparkledust
It is time for spring to arrive in Little Blossoming but there is
a problem and winter is staying put. Can Felicity Wishes get
the seasons back on track?

Felicity Wishes: Secrets and Surprises

Felicity Wishes is planning her birthday party but it seems none of her friends can come. Will Felicity end up celebrating her birthday alone?

Felicity Wishes: Friendship and Fairyschool

It's nearly time for Felicity Wishes to leave fairyschool, but she has no idea what kind of fairy she wants to be. Will Felicity find her true talent?

Felicity Wishes has lots to say in these fantastic little books:

Little Book of Friendship

Little Book of Birthdays

Little Book of Wishes

Little Book of Happiness

Little Book of Love

Little Book of Peace

Little Book of Hiccups

Little Book of Every Day Wishes

Little Book of Fun